&

WILD SEEDS

Wild Seeds

&

Francis Rothluebber

New Momentum

New Momentum
P.O. Box 807
Idyllwild, CA 92549

Rothluebber, Francis
    Wild Seeds / Francis Rothluebber
    ISBN 978-1-4507-1852-3

A poem is always a surprise.

Contents

1   Part One

5   There is a word that never ends
7   The great Spanish Teresa said
9   Tell me, Divine One
11   Meditation
13   You must love music, Beloved
15   Each day a new word
17   I watch the flame of the breakfast candle
19   I long to see the Face of Light
21   How do you make love with the Spirit
23   Why ever did you trust us with the Earth
25   Love has many languages, Beloved
27   I thought I was hearing a sound
29   I hold the familiar book for a moment
31   We are conceived in the Consciousness
33   The Sages tell us

35   Part Two

39   It is a live poem
41   The crumb was three times his size
43   Mountain, you are a special friend
45   Sun
47   "The Tamil language is very precise"
49   If wood could sing
51   This small second-floor deck is an incubating nest
53   A mountain invites the eye
55   Good morning, Ocean Stone
57   My oldest sister, Moon
59   Never say a mountain is a mountain
61   My soul found a new cousin
63   The eye is never filled with seeing
65   The salt danced out of the shaker
67   Just before the sun
69   Dawn lifts its face from the darkness

71   Part Three

75   A poem is often a metaphor
77   I am in a Wind dance
79   Come, marvel at the word
81   Strange
83   If I were given a vase
85   I would join the madly-in-love outrageous
87   Can one eat silence?
89   A fitting image of my relationship with You
91   "If I could step out of my body"
93   I am not sure what David felt
95   Sweet solitude can be a sweet singing Lorelei
97   Somewhere down the way I will meet myself
99   There is no hole in the Universe
101   Silence is a paradox
103   The path between speaking and silence

A poem is a seed the wind drops when it will.

Between a sip of coffee and the swallow,
between the leap of a squirrel
and the fall of a pine cone,
a poem can fly in.

Forced to open,
so sensitive is this seed,
it is deformed.

Left too long
untended
it disappears.

What mind does the wind obey
when it drops a surprise seed?

What strange land does this seed come from?

This seed always brings a breath of ecstasy.

Introductory Note

A poem is always a surprise. I have never experienced one to arrive "on demand."

I had not received a poem for a long stretch of time, probably because I have been involved in the study of Eastern wisdom writings, especially those of Sri Aurobindo, and, also, in creating several series of guided meditations and workshops to help release the power in these writings.

Recently, however, a sudden flurry of poems, like wild seeds, has arrived.

I don't think of a poem as mine. I feel I am a servant to it, giving it a visible body so the sweet fire that is sleeping in the "seed" can break free.

I never feel I own a poem, or at least only partly own a poem since I participate in shaping it.

A poem comes to be shared. So if any poem or line catches hold in you, make it yours. It was meant for you.

Several creative friends have helped to put this collection of poems in your hands. The first is Wanie Reeverts, who has created the "seed" paintings. Her work is always a visual proof of Monet's thought: "Everything is an envelope for light."

The second is Elaine Hirschenberger, who prepared this material for publication. Elaine is director of Womanspace, a center for women in Rockford, Illinois, empowering women in all possibilities.

The third is Cookie Anderson, who, with her financial assistance, made this sowing of the seeds possible.

Here is a pocketful of warm seeds. They are dedicated to you.

PART ONE

The seed of God is in me.
Now the seed of a pear tree
grows into a pear tree;

a hazel seed into a hazel tree;

the seed of God into God.

Meister Eckhart

&

There is a word that never ends:
"Become."

The sound of this word is carried
second by second
in the Creating Breath,
delicate,
Kabir says.
as the sound of the ant's ankle bracelet.
Powerful.
It is the first sound that is always beginning.

The seed hears it and stirs.
The plant listens for it
to know the time for the yellow pansy to open.
The egg hears it
and the wet chick knocks on the shell.
The wren catches it
and tries a first vibrating trill.
The child hears it and laughs
discovering the dog's ear.

Everything that is,
the Universe itself,
listens and keeps
awakening.

Even on the other side
of death
we will hear Love say,
"Become."

The great Spanish Teresa said,
(I think she lifted her eyebrows as she said)
"Any concept of God is a jar to be broken."

We used to break jars as the centuries turned:
       the warrior God
       the judge God
       the distant creator God
Then we broke jars in shorter centuries:
       the father God
       the mother God
       the no-gender God
We tried the no-parenting jars:
       The Verb
       The Ground
       The Source
In recent short decades the jars became porous:
       pure vibrating Sea of Energy
       vast Darkness that is Pure Light
       the Evolutionary Urging
Last year
       the one Shining Breath hidden in everything
Yesterday
       the pulsing electric Presence

Today, for a second, there is no jar
       only a wild, free, joy
       One
       You

Tell me, Divine One,
        do you love to dance?

    I see you as the First Sufi
        whirling tirelessly,
        galaxy after galaxy,
        spinning, spinning,
        never falling,
        wild with love of Your creating.

    How can I dance with You
        unless you carry me?

Meditation.

You sway us
            in the cradle of Your breath
            from earth to stars
            from night to dawn
            from time to now.

We listen and rest
            in Your "I am here" mantra.

We rise and follow
            the echo within us.

You must love music, Beloved.

Ten thousand master drums
      thunder forth the opening
      of Your creation symphony
      each second.

Then silence.

Then every being swells
      the great OM symphony,
      from the whispery oboe note of every insect
      to the deep cello of every mountain.

Then silence.

The dissonance and cacophony.
We ache and we long for the pure harmonic note
      of Your human family.

Each day a new word
        becomes a silken tether
        to help a wandering mind find home
        or to guide it from the busyness fog
        back to center.

But today, I listened for the word.

Today, but today,
        a full voice, a mountain bell
        in the deepest canyon
        keeps ringing:

I Am the Word.

I watch the flame of the breakfast candle
        stretch.

I know the feeling.

Live my life with me,
        I pray.

From a depth I cannot fathom
        I hear:

"Live My Life with Me."

        Ah!

I long to see the Face of Light.

I would slit the invisible glass shield that hides You.
I know, I know, I cannot look into the face of the sun
        without going blind.

How then could I see Your Face?

For a single glimpse
I would gladly walk blind
Feeling the warmth
        of You.

How can I see Your Face
when You are looking through my eyes?

How do you make love with the Spirit,

the Divine Spirit?

You share one breath,

You share one energy,

You share one creating.

Open. Receiving. Radiating,

One.

"You look as if you just made love," she said.

Why ever did You trust us with the Earth,
Your jewel, Your pearl of great price?

Why did You trust us with Water,
pure crystal in the sunlight?

With rain-forests
lush with table-sized leaves?

What do You see in us?

Love has many languages, Beloved.

Sometimes Your whisper
is a soft mist on the face of my heart.
I hurry on.
I have missed it.

Sometimes when I am unsure
in the daytime fog
Your word is a warm hand on my shoulder.
I trust,
The way opens.

Sometimes Your word
is the sharp snap of a fall on ice.
Sudden.
All my careful plans lie splintered.
Why? I listen.
Is this word really yours?

Sometimes when day
is about to open the door from sleep,
Your word, full Light, breaks in,
sets my personal planet spinning in a new direction.
Certain.
"It is finished."

I thought I was hearing a sound
from a nearby room
to my right.

Only there is no room.

A patient sound of someone
trying to open a door
that keeps being sucked shut.

Is it a door of a room inside me?
A silent space I have as yet not entered.

Or is it a door to a vast room all around me?
where pain is seeking compassion.

Or is it, is it,
a door to a limitless room,
a Presence

I hold the familiar book for a moment.

Suddenly I know why the Torah
was wrapped in exquisite cloth
woven with gold threads.

My hands grow warm.

Today You would speak words
soaking deep into my heart.

Today my life may take a new direction.
Totally new.

We are conceived in the Consciousness
            we name "God."
We are chosen, known.

From this Womb there is no birth.
We will never be born nor separated.

In this Womb we partner
            in a vibrating dance,
            a pulsing dance,
            an alive dance
            a revealing dance.

Strange Womb --
            exquisite, radiant Stillness.

The sages tell us
        to be mindful
        of the space between the inbreath
        and the outbreath.

I ask why.
        I know we cannot keep drinking and drinking in
        breath;
        we would implode.
        I know we cannot keep expelling and expelling
        breath;
        we would collapse.

What is happening in this space?
        A little death?
        A tiny second of nothing?

No, no.

Here is a miniature opening
        to the Ocean,
        that is All Breath
        upon which the breath tides
ride.

PART TWO

We cannot sow seeds with clenched fists.

To sow we must open our hands.

Adolfo Perez Esquivel

It is a live poem
to watch the silent power of water
wash the face of a stone.

Dry, chalky, asleep,
the snoozing stone wakes.

Colors explode
Veins vibrate.

The stone soul shines through.

The crumb was three times his size.
This ant was on a line-drive
to that circle of red sands
and the open door down.

Did he hear the hummingbird whirr en route?
Did he see that single blue-purple surprise in the grass?
He did not stop once to rest his tiny back.

I could sense ant commitment!
ant passion!

     Not for me today.
     Today I am putting my crumb down.

There is a white gold Light shimmering in everything.

Mountain, you are a special friend.

You sit like an ancient Buddha,
       still and awake
       letting the wind carve your face
       allowing the snow to rest on your head.

I sit at your feet
       sharing my expectations
       complaining of my disappointments.

I hear your invitation:

"Use me as your mirror."

Sun,
you are indeed faithful,
        would I were so.
I wander off in a fog
that is neither day nor night.

The Prophet put words
into your hot mouth:
        "I am at home;
            you are in the faraway places."

I am in a faraway cloud of busy dust.

"The Tamil language is very precise,"
the Tamil Poet said.
"There are seven different words
between the English words, 'bud' and 'flower'."

One would have to live in attentive quiet,
live with the plant,
marvelling at each subtle change
to create such a language.

Love creates such a language.

If wood could sing?

Indeed, it does.
Walk, listening.

An oak bass,
An alto willow,
even the boy soprano of a new spruce.

A sweet murmur rises in the heart of tree after tree:

"Alive! Alive."

This small second-floor deck is an incubating nest.

If you walk out, sit down, feeling limp and gray,
        the work you had set your mind to create
        is tasting flat and dull,
you will find the cedars are waiting.

These cedars are old enough
        to be shedding ribbons of bark.
They are great ladies, friends.
They will quietly spin and spin energy into you
        and astonish you:

"You have been about the wrong project,
        the one your busy mind selected."

A new project bursts open.

Without thought your body bows to them
        as you stand to leave,
        your pulse electric.

A mountain invites the eye.

Where the eye goes the heart follows.

Within the heart a mystical mountain grows:
      sure, serene, alive.

Good morning, Ocean Stone,

You have been a faithful paper-weight
        for a hundred months.

This morning, I saw you for the first time,
        saw your blue-black rings
        and your light gray circles.

Amazing.

How old are you?
How did you acquire such beauty
        in the bottom of the ocean?
How many waves have you surfed
        to float free?

I look for the Invisible Light
        holding you together.

Perhaps it is good I cannot see It;
I would have to live this day on my knees.

My oldest sister, Moon,
       uses Clearwater Lake
      for her looking-glass.

I watched Moon in the water
      chuckle.

Never say a mountain is a mountain
        is a mountain.

The mountains in Palm Springs
        arch up their backs
        straight from the level ground.

The mountains of Arizona
        stretch out their muscles
        and lie along the horizon in the heat.

The mountains of Utah
        after a night rain
        become red glass in the morning.

And my mountain, my mountain at dawn
        stands erect, covered with snow-ice,
        live coals shimmering.

My soul found a new cousin,
  a picture of a new cousin,
  on a card from a friend.

In a red-orange sky
  that is mirrored in a red lake
  a majestic loon,
   black against the red
  expands its power wings,
  arches its throat in a longing delight

as it lifts off into a yellow sun.

The eye is never filled with seeing;

The empty ear waits for sound.

The heart is never filled with loving.

We are designed to be

s p a c e

The salt danced out of the shaker
onto my perfect egg
too fast.

I can not return salt back to the shaker.
Ask Lot's wife.
What was her name?
She looked back, through tears perhaps.
A pillar of salt.

The blocks of salt near my grandfather's barn
had concave hollows where the horses licked deep into the salt.
He said, "Salt is good for them"

I eat my egg
trying not to look back and back and back.

Today this egg is good for me.

Just before the sun
        splashed
over the mountain,
the light changed the trees
        on the rim
into a crystal fringe.

I would have my
        death
be such a moment.

Dawn lifts its face from the darkness
        The birds tune a bit
        and burst into full orchestra.

Peace lifts its face from the conflict.
        All around the world
        hearts stand still.

Forgiveness lifts its face from the resentment.
        Life comes unstuck
        and flows freely in the current.

PART THREE

First there must be
the desire;
that desire is the seed
from which transformation
grows.
This seed within us
waits in stillness.

Julia Butterfly Hill

&

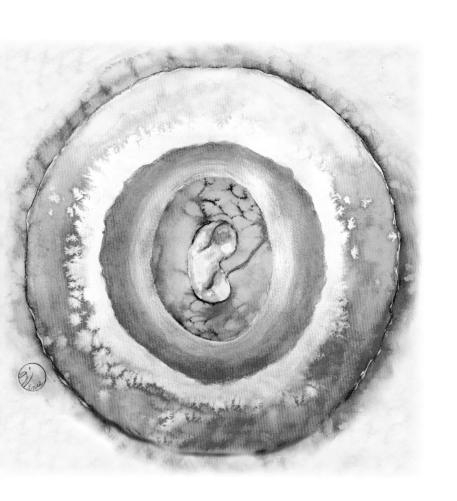

A poem is often a metaphor;
        one experience lighting up another.

Sometimes after a long journey
        when the bodymind is sitting quiet
        it feels as if it is still moving.

This bodymind is moving.
These conscious cells have been on a journey
        for fourteen billion years.
These cells have experienced
        floating in the ocean
        leading a root into the earth
        winging off a branch
        putting the fourth foot down
        standing upright
and since there is only one mind
        stepping on the moon.

At this moment the conscious cells in all bodyminds are traveling.
Meditators can feel these cells are on their way to the real
        authentic Eden
                where all are in a virtual hug
                loved and loving.

This poem is no metaphor.

I am in a Wind dance.

The Living Breath inside my breath
        leads surprisingly.

I decide to settle down, retire,
rest like a leaf that is finished.
No, I am picked up, waltzed,
and gently placed in a new garden to take new root.

Yesterday,
the Wind scooped me up
like a house of sand in the desert,
whirled me in a wild tango,
scattering my carefully designed image of my success.

Yesterday, I thought I was a failure.
Today, I discover a hidden spring of true water.

Come, marvel at the word,
　　　"Nevertheless."
Strange word and powerful.

This word is a swinging door.

On one side sit nine justices,
　　　real or imagined,
putting their judgments
and expectations on your life.

Stand in the doorway.
　　　Listen inside for your heart message.
　　　Choose.

"Nevertheless."

Swing the door open.
Enter the vast home of Light and Peace.

Strange.
I think when I use a word
I know
what I am saying.

I see a circle of melting snow
around a fresh lemon crocus
I cup my hand over it
to feel the warmth
"It's alive."

Life

An annoying squirrel
is practicing aerobics
digging in the wet earth
flipping out the roots
of the primrose I just planted.
I forgive.
"We share life."

Life

I fall through the word
into what
depth?

If I were given a vase,
   ancient, worth thousands,
I would marvel at the artist,
   lost in a long-ago century,
   who loved it into being.

I would place it in the finest light
   to reveal its exquisite design.

I would greet it reverently,
   a new feast each morning
   for my eyes and heart.

But now I just saw you.

I would join the madly-in-love outrageous,
those who rub meat on the walls of the hut in Assisi
because it is Christmas:
"Love is here and nothing should be hungry."

Those who toss flowers so abundant in Calcutta
at the walls and the serving bowls
because it is Spring and
"Sacred Life is here."

Those who sit silently in a cave near Arunachula
for sixteen years
ignoring the biting insects
because the whisper in the depths is so deep
"The taste of that music is ever-changing delicious."

Can one eat silence?

I know one can eat black silence,
the dreaded fear of dropping into the abyss
in the night.
The body unable to breathe with this food.

Perhaps a memory
of a near-death in the womb.

Can one eat silence?

I keep nibbling at the edges of this bread,
a substantial, nourishing food
that feels as if true sun-energy lives in this bread.
This bread creates a hunger.

But the whole loaf?
That seems to demand no other food be eaten?

Perhaps a fast before the rich food
that is coming.

A fitting image of my relationship with You,
        Divine One,
is the weaving of a cheesecloth
with the gaping holes of my forgetfulness.

Yesterday, a mindless moving through activities,
        unaware of Your Presence.

Today, You assure me,
        Generous One,
this is human weaving,
this is the nature of a cheesecloth.

We are one.
The cloth continues.
Begin again
and again.

"If I could step out of my body"

No, no!
If I could step into my body,
sink down,
down into the marrow of my bones,
I could hear what rocks and mountains are saying to us.

If I could spin down,
down into my blood,
let the cells open their hearts,
I could learn how the rivers,
how the water in this glass and my shower
want to dance with me.

If I could seep down,
down into the Light pulsing in my breath
I could hear the conversation of birds,
the whispers of the stars
in our shared body.

And I would know
         as love knows,
you.

I am not sure what David felt
stepping out with slingshot and stone.

I know how I feel in front of the stranglehold
     of munition makers,
     of pharmaceutical companies,
     the money Goliaths oppressing the powerless.

I know the stone and the skilled arm alone
did not bring down the blind giant, boasting and righteous.

But the One who can, does not without the stone and the arm
and the heart of a David.

Yes, sometimes without the stone and the skill
but never without the heart.

Sweet Solitude can be a sweet singing Lorelei.

My small boat drifting in the current,
Quiet, quiet.
Only an occasional cloud,
        an occasional oar lapping the water,
        an occasional gull making its awkward landing.
I smile.

Sweet Solitude has another song.

The current churns into whitewater,
the boat hangs on the stone cliff,
spins upside down, cutting the turbulence.

Mind muscle,
heart muscle,
trust muscle,
stretch
clinging.

Somewhere down the way I will meet myself.
    My Self.

All along I have been taking off heavy ego-coats
    that weigh me down.
I think I have dropped them one by one
    only to find each time I have woven
    a subtler, finer-textured tunic.

I am learning to forget coats and tunics
    and simply breathe in Light
    until every vein and muscle and bone
    is alive, glows with Light.

And I walk, a breathing alabaster presence,
    my Self.

There is no hole in the Universe.

In this one vast weaving of myriad-colored,
      multi-layered Light threads
      I often think of myself as a french knot
      or a dropped stitch.

There is no unravelling here.

The Great Heart of the Universe
      spinning out the Light threads
      keeps knitting me in.

Now I feel the tiniest tug
      and the agony of torturous human snarls

as mine.

Silence is a paradox.

Silence lures us away from sounds
      to listen to a deeper Sound.

Silence withdraws us into an empty womb
      to find we are pregnant with All.

Silence creates an inner space of darkness
      that suddenly is filled with Light

Silence feeds an empty hunger
      that nourishes us beyond the richest taste.

The path between speaking and silence
            is a railroad track.
Either choice could cause a collision.

Speaking could set a careening train
            speeding into a jungle ravine.
Silence could stop a moving train
            like a boulder in a tunnel.

I am learning to slow down the train
            and follow an inner sight
            around the risky turn.